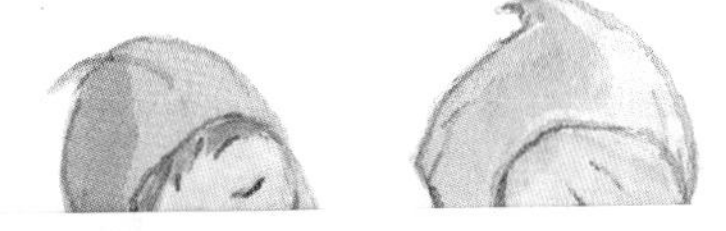

TOM FINGER

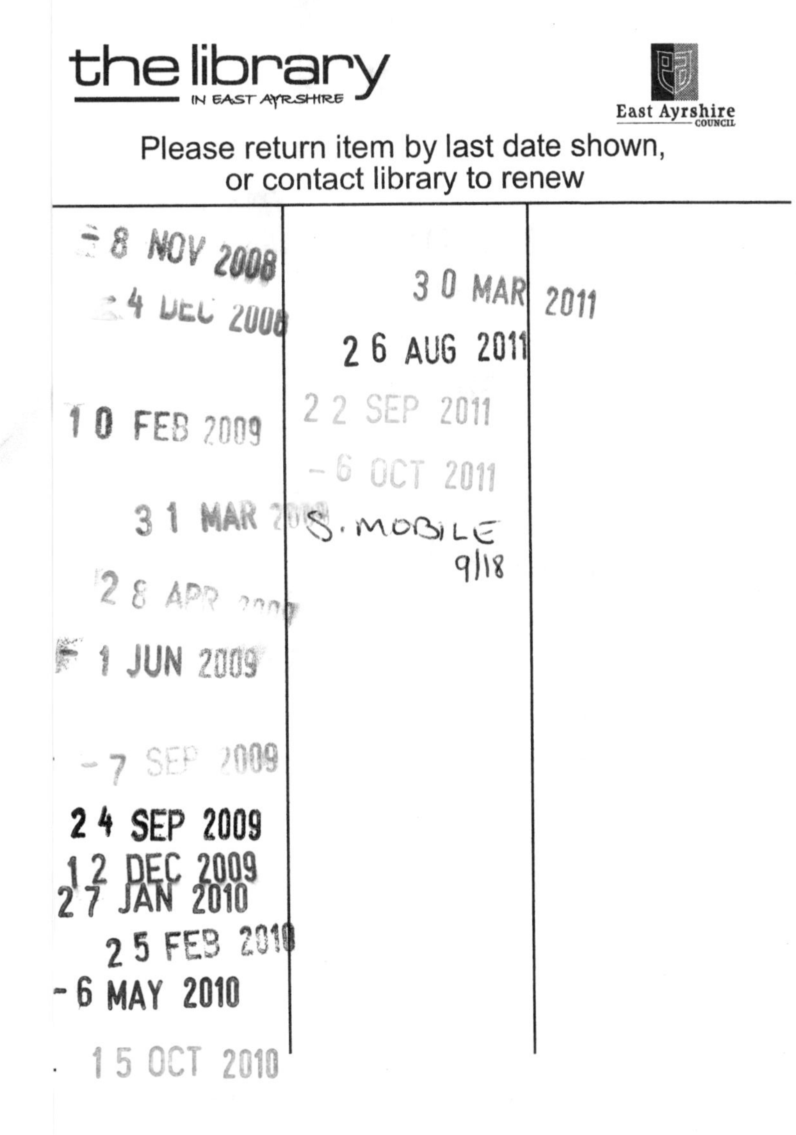

For Richard, George and Jack – GM^cC

First published in Great Britain in 2001 by Bloomsbury Publishing Plc
38 Soho Square, London, W1D 3HB
This paperback edition first published in 2002

A CIP catalogue record of this book is available from the British Library
ISBN 0 7475 5596 6

Designed by Sarah Hodder
Printed in Hong Kong by South China Printing Co.

1 3 5 7 9 10 8 6 4 2

There was once a little girl called Queenie who had a dear Tabby cat. One winter Queenie's Tabby cat died of old age.

Every day Queenie called her Tabby, sadly she called her dear old Tabby. But Queenie's brother Ben said,

'Stop calling your Tabby, he won't come back!'

Again on Monday Queenie called her Tabby, sadly she called her dear old Tabby, but he didn't come back. Instead, in walked another Tabby cat, in from the cold. He was young, he was bold and his eyes were bright blue.

'You're not my Tabby, my dear old Tabby. Who are you?' Queenie said.

'Tom Finger,' this bold young Tabby replied.

'And where do you come from, Young Tabby Tom Finger?' Queenie asked.

'Somewhere spooky,' Queenie's brother Ben cried. In a blinking Tom Finger was gone.

On Tuesday, Queenie called her Tabby, sadly she called her dear old Tabby, but he didn't come back. Instead, in walked Young Tabby Tom Finger, in from the cold and laid a lace handkerchief on Queenie's chair. Then Tom Finger smiled at Queenie with his bright blue eyes.

'Thank you, Tom Finger, but whose cat are you?' asked Queenie.

'A witch's cat!' Ben cried and in a blinking Tom Finger was gone.

'No, his eyes are too blue,' Queenie said as she looked at the footprints out in the snow. But where did he come from and where did he go?

She'd never know, for his footprints didn't stay.
Queenie watched them melt away.

On Wednesday, Queenie was about to call her Tabby, her dear old Tabby, when in walked Tom Finger, in from the cold and laid a satin soap bag in Queenie's lap. Then Tom Finger smiled at Queenie with his bright blue eyes.

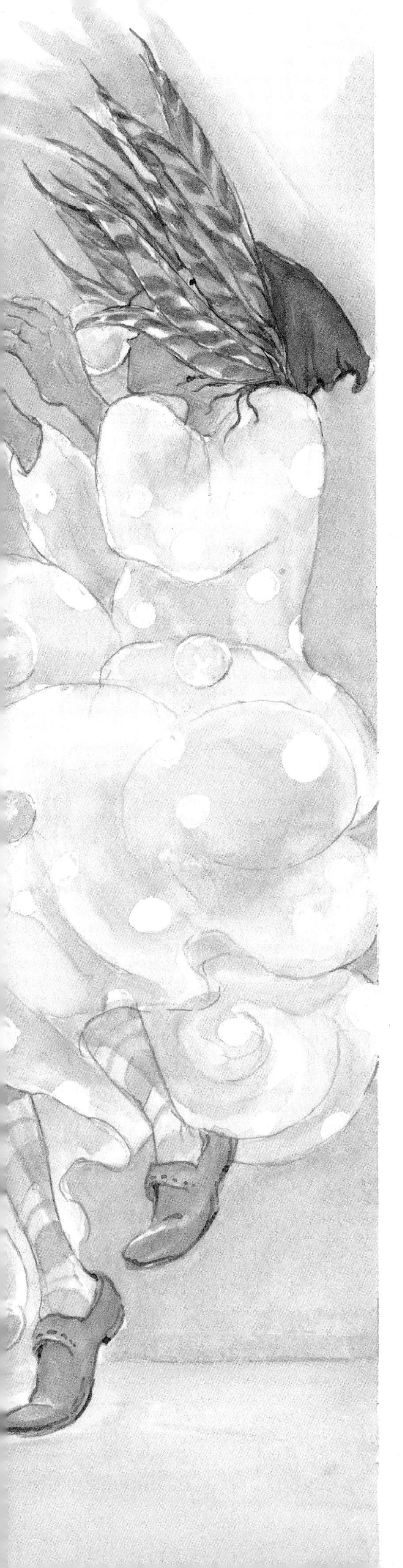

'Thank you, Tom Finger, but is this a soap bag?' asked Queenie.

'It's one of the witch's magic things,' Ben said. *'Now she'll blow soap suds into your eyes,'* and in a blinking Tom Finger was gone.

'No, that is all lies,' Queenie said as she looked at the footprints melting in the snow. 'But, Young Tabby Tom Finger, where do you come from and where do you go?'

On Thursday, before Queenie could call her Tabby, in walked Young Tabby Tom Finger, in from the cold and laid a silk slipper at Queenie's feet. Then Tom Finger smiled at Queenie with his bright blue eyes.

'Thank you, Tom Finger, but whose slipper is this?' Queenie asked.

'Another of the witch's magic things,' Ben said. *'Her slippery slipper. It will trip you up!'* In a blinking, Tom Finger was gone.

'No, that can't be so,' Queenie said, as she looked at the footprints out in the snow. 'But, Young Tabby Tom Finger, will I ever know where it is you come from and where it is you go?'

On Friday, in walked Young Tabby Tom Finger, in from the cold and placed an embroidered needlecase in Queenie's hand. Then Tom Finger smiled at Queenie with his bright blue eyes.

'Thank you, Tom Finger, but why do you bring me an embroidered needlecase?' asked Queenie.

'He's brought you the witch's magic needles,' Ben said. *'Now she'll make a snare and trap you there!'* In a blinking Tom Finger was gone.

'Nonsense!' Queenie said as she looked at the footprints out in the snow.

'But, Young Tabby Tom Finger, why won't you tell me where it is you come from and where it is you go?'

On Sunday, Queenie waited and waited, but nothing walked in from the cold. So Queenie called Tom Finger, sadly she called Young Tabby Tom Finger, but he didn't come back. His footprints were lost in the snow.

Then Queenie picked up the lace handkerchief, the satin soap bag and silk slipper. She picked up the embroidered needlecase and the unfinished shawl.

'I must look for Tom Finger and bring him back these things,' Queenie said to Ben, who was sitting by the fire. 'Will you come with me?'

But he shook his
head and said, 'No fear,
I'm staying here.'
'Then I'll go alone,' and
Queenie followed the wool that led
from the shawl across the floor and out
of the door. Out of the door and into the cold.

All alone, Queenie followed the wool over the snow and up a high hill hidden in cloud, where the sky filled with snowflakes and Queenie couldn't see.

Then Queenie was afraid. So she stroked the satin soap bag and called to Tom Finger with his bright blue eyes. Sadly she called,

'Young Tabby Tom Finger, I'm bringing back these things, but I'm lost in the snow and can't see where to go.'

In a blinking, the snowflakes stopped falling. Queenie could see.

'Thank you, Tom Finger,' Queenie said. 'Now I know you can hear, so I've nothing to fear,' and the wool in the snow showed her which way to go.

All alone, Queenie
followed the wool
over the snow and
down a deep dell,
frozen so hard that
the ground turned
to ice and Queenie
slipped and fell.
Then Queenie
was afraid.

So she stroked the silk slipper and called to Tom Finger with his bright blue eyes. Sadly she called, 'Young Tabby Tom Finger, I'm bringing back these things, but I've slipped in the snow and don't know where to go.'

In a blinking, the ice was gone and Queenie could stand.

'Thank you, Tom Finger. Now I've nothing to fear. The wool keeps leading on, but I know the end is near.'

All alone, Queenie followed the wool over the snow and into a wood all prickly and thick, where the branches had thorns and Queenie got caught.

Then Queenie was afraid. So she stroked the embroidered needlecase and called to Tom Finger with his bright blue eyes. Sadly she called,

'Young Tabby Tom Finger, I'm bringing back these things, but I'm trapped in the snow and don't know where to go.'

In a blinking, the thorns were gone and Queenie was free.

'Thank you, Tom Finger. Now I've nothing to fear, for the end of the wool can't be far from here.'

All alone, Queenie followed the wool over the snow until the end was in sight. And there stood a house with its door open wide and waiting outside …

Young Tabby Tom Finger! He stood at the door with the end of the wool held in his paw. Queenie waved to Tom Finger.

'So this is where you come from and this is where you go!'

Tom Finger smiled at Queenie with his bright blue eyes and a voice from inside cried,

'Tom Finger, Tom Finger, bring her in from the cold!'

Queenie was afraid.

Tom Finger led Queenie in through the door and an old blind woman shuffled over the floor.

'I can no longer see, bring her to me,' she said.

'I've brought you back your things,' Queenie said.
The old blind woman stroked them.
'My precious things,' she cried.

'The little lace hanky I had as a child, the satin soap bag I took out into the world. The darling silk slipper I wore as a bride, the needlecase I embroidered with my needles safe inside. And you've brought back the shawl,' the old woman sighed, 'the shawl left unfinished when my dear husband died.'

Then the old woman smiled at Queenie with her old blind eyes.

'I'll get you a surprise,' she said, 'for bringing back my things,' and she wrapped something small in the unfinished shawl... Queenie peeped inside.

'Oh!' Queenie cried, 'You've given me a kitten, a dear little kitty, just like my Tabby, but with bright blue eyes!'

'Now you must go,' the old woman said, 'Tom Finger will lead you, back through the snow.'

Tom Finger led Queenie safely back home.

Ben was waiting out in the snow. He was worried and said,
'When you followed the wool to the very end, did you find a witch?'
'Not a witch, just a friend. She gave me a kitten with bright blue eyes.'
Queenie turned to Tom Finger,
'Isn't that so?'

But Tom Finger had gone. In a blinking he'd gone.
Not even his footprints were left in the snow.